The Dark Path of Our Names

Other Books by Joan Swift

Poetry

THIS ELEMENT (1965)

PARTS OF SPEECH (1978)

History

BRACKETT'S LANDING (1975)

The Dark Path
of Our Names

Joan Swift

Dragon Gate, Inc.

© 1985 by Joan Swift. All rights reserved.

Designed by Tree Swenson.
The type is Stempel Garamond.
Cover image from "The Visitor" series by Paul Marioni, blown
and flattened glass, 1984; photographed by Roger Schreiber.

Library of Congress Cataloging in Publication Data

Swift, Joan.
    The dark path of our names.

    I. Title.
PS3569.W5D3   1985   811'.54   85-1465
ISBN 0-937872-26-1
ISBN 0-937872-27-X (pbk.)

Dragon Gate, Inc., 508 Lincoln Street
Port Townsend, Washington 98368

Acknowledgments

Grateful acknowledgment is made to the following publications in which some of these poems first appeared: *American Poetry Review*, "His Sister"; *The Antioch Review*, "Charms against Bears," "The Horses at Hanagita," "Night Flying"; *The Chowder Review*, "Ermine," "Her Husband"; *The Iowa Review*, "My Grandmother's Hair," "Father," "Pneumonia," "1933"; *King County Arts*, "Northern Lights," "Orchids"; *The Montana Review*, "Diggers at Langley," "Wait for Heaven"; *Poetry-In-Motion*, Seattle, "Tebay Lake" (titled "Lake"); *Poetry Northwest*, "Silent," "Strip Mining, Antrim Cemetery," "Poem," "Ravine," "Coroner," "Beside Her Husband," "Her Husband to Himself," "Prisoner"; *Seattle Review*, "Spider." "My Grandmother's Hair," "Father," "1933," "Pneumonia" were reprinted in *Extended Outlooks: The Iowa Review Collection of Contemporary Women Writers*, Macmillan, 1982. "Diggers at Langley" and "Father" were reprinted in *Rain in the Forest, Light in the Trees: Contemporary Poetry from the Northwest*, Owl Creek Press, 1983. "The Alphabet of Coal" won the Poetry Society of America's Lucille Medwick Memorial Award for 1982.

Without the help of Deputy District Attorney Rockne Harmon of the Alameda County, California, District Attorney's office and Art Guzman, Inspector with that office, many of the poems in Section Two of this book could not have been written. My thanks also to Bill and Nancy Whelan and Pat and Maryanne Gipson for their generosity and support.

I am indebted to the National Endowment for the Arts for a fellowship in 1982, which enabled me to complete this work.

Both the author and the publisher wish to express their gratitude to the King County, Washington, Arts Commission for a generous publication grant in 1984, and to the Literature Program of the National Endowment for the Arts for additional grant support which greatly assisted the publication of this book.

for Gwen Head and Sandra McPherson...

with affection

CONTENTS

One

3   Father

4   1933

5   Pneumonia

6   My Grandmother's Hair

7   Wait for Heaven

8   The Alphabet of Coal

10   Strip Mining, Antrim Cemetery

11   Operation

13   Orchids

14   The Horses at Hanagita

15   Northern Lights

16   Charms against Bears

18   Ermine

20   Tebay Lake

21   Diggers at Langley

23   Poem

24   Silent

25   Ultraviolet

26   Spider

28   Night Flying

29   Gourds

30   Voyage

31   When You Play in the Undertow

Two:
Testimony

35 Ravine

36 Coroner

37 Her Husband

38 Victim

39 Beside Her Husband

40 Her Husband, to Himself

41 His Mother

43 His Sister

44 D'Lo, *de l'Eau*

45 Another Witness

49 Detective

50 Prisoner

One

Father

In the dining room painting of my childhood
the sheep are lost in a blizzard.
Against wild roses, they lean brown wool to brown wool
under the snow's diagonal.
The flakes gather in furrows on their coats
like a field where nothing is planted yet.
Their hooves disappear and all the soft parts
between their front legs and their back legs
are buried in weather.

Sheep can't say *cold* or *alone* or *save me*.
They can't say *where is the shepherd?*
A horse stamps in a barn somewhere not in the painting.
At the edges the sky is black and the center is blacker.
The sheep close their eyes against the wind.
For years they are closed.

Waiting for them to open in a bewilderment of spring
flowers, I drink snow milk   snow milk.

I wait forever.

1933

The saw gleams in her hand like a cat's teeth,
dangerous light in the black cellar.
In her other hand, one leg of the oak table.

It is winter again and a cold house...
ten days since you came with any kind of kiss
for us or your arms swinging.

Now my mother begins the strange music.
She is holding the table like a cello or a baby.
She leans to the need with her difficult bow.

The legs go in through the furnace door.
The wild grain crackles.
Flames dance on the oval top in orange shoes.

It is not a table anymore, a place for the lamp,
three rings, and a gouge in the finish
where you threw the glass

and she sat crying. Only this heat,
a smell like nutmeg, smoke drawn up the chimney,
you drifting away.

Pneumonia

The year of my mother's divorce
snow lay at the back door like a great hound.
The potatoes closed all their eyes in the root cellar.
I wore a patched coat to school, brown stockings.
I stepped in the bigger steps and carried
my hunger in wool hands.
But nothing was warm enough.
A draft blew in and out somewhere around my heart.

When it was time, they put my sickness
on a small cot near the potbellied stove.
Eight days I lay in fever,
one hundred five, one hundred six...
Sunny, sunny, I said.
And my hands climbed all over the wallpaper
to gather the yellow day lilies,
the cut stems.

My Grandmother's Hair

She wanted to arrive in heaven with beautiful hair,
coppery glow, chestnut haloes of rectitude.
Milking the cows at dawn, it was yesterday's braids
she felt rocking against her cheeks, her head bent,
the pail giving back its metallic song.

So when they brought her home dead from the Blossburg hospital,
my mother brushed down from the cold scalp for hours.
Hair fanned out like a brown waterfall over the gray end of the coffin.

Lifting the head was hardest, to stroke each strand
and twine it in place.
She combed by kerosene lamplight.
When morning came and neighbors to the parlor door,
three circles shone on my grandmother's head.

Pink roses lay on the gray velvet,
each one letting a curl of pink ribbon down
with another rose knotted at the end....

Kiss her goodbye, my mother said.

The stool was dark and embroidered.
When my lips touched the rigid cheek,
the finest of hairs, the little unmanageable wisps near the hairline,
brushed my face.

Wait for Heaven

The windows are clear because the congregation is poor.
But over the cross one pane brims with sun so everything
                                                    turns gold:
the minister's hair, one black side of the Bible,
dust in the air.

The miners are singing.
En morgon jag i himlen vakna får.
En morgon glad hos Frälseran där hemma.
The words rise over the black suits and ties
under their chins like goiters.

In the morning I will wake up in heaven.
But my grandmother lies under the slag of the gray casket,
her head not tilting as it did among the peonies.
Other milkers and sewers are taking the high notes.

My cousin sucks his fist.
His fingers are webbed with saliva.
If I lean forward in the pew
I can almost see the stairway
the voices are building out of the coal mines.

Förbida Herran, tiden är så kort.
A bird flies past the window, red under its wings.
Wait for the Lord. Time is short.
It flies past in a second.

All those years my grandfather hung his watch
on a nail beside their bed.
While they slept it kept time in the dark.

The Alphabet of Coal

This is my grandfather working his stall in the mine.
This is the sky where stars come down on a pick.

> *Anchor, Aztec, Beacon, Big Horn,*
> *Black Beauty, Chanticleer, Chinook,*

Under the green earth runs a black vein.
This is the dynamite, this is the tamping stick.

> *Diamond Glo, Dixie Star, Enos, Fire Chief,*
> *Grey Eagle, Hanna, Hedlite, Hiawatha,*

Under the green earth the first blue crocuses start.
This is his hand, the fuse, and the explosion.

> *Imperial, Inferno, Jewell Pocahontas,*
> *Kincaid, Lehigh Valley, Lone Star, Maiden,*

And my grandmother standing at the weathered gate.
This is my grandfather walking alone.

> *Marianna, Meltwell, Mountaineer,*
> *Old Abe, Old Ben, Orient, Power King,*

There is a stone in his left hand or a dead thrush.
In his right hand there is red.

> *Quick Heat, Randall, Raven, Roberta,*
> *Royal Smokeless, Scarlet Flame,*

This is the needle pulling flesh to flesh.
Black fingers, black blood.

> *Stonega, Tennessee Jewell, Tiger,*
> *Violet, Virglow, Volunteer, White Flame,*

Under the earth lie all the syllables.
These are the ashes sifting through the grate.

> *Winding Gulf, Wingfoot, Yellow Jacket,*
> *Yellow Glo, Zulu.*

This is my grandfather reading the Swedish Bible.
These are the stubs. These are the words he can't write.

Strip Mining, Antrim Cemetery

Through the ore of autumn, toward the stone angel
with outstretched arms, the draglines are moving.
How many seasons they have worked near the graveyard,
gouging the earth for its darkness. The shovels
make a range of jagged mountains and a canyon
deep enough for hell. This was a meadow. Sorrel
grew over coal. This was a forest. And the miners
are trapped in the same night with its hard stars
all over again. Their knucklebones shine
in the bituminous, the spaces between their ribs
fill with black dust, they who dreamed of death
as release, who dug toward a light heaven,
whose voices are still now under the draglines.

Operation

Laying me down on the kitchen table
when I was five, my uncle
who was a doctor took my tonsils out.
Later, the aunt who owned it,
not his wife, another aunt
who was stitching up the cut
of my mother's separation
gave me the table.
I was lately married, thought
I could write my own new story
on the white enamel top:

> "They painted their kitchen yellow.
>   When the sun came in the window,
>   it was like living inside a buttercup."

Or

> "She set out the strawberry plates,
>   forks, spoons. In the middle, soufflé —
>   the golden rising of their single being."

Or

> "The smell of laundry dried in wind
>   pleased her. She folded white towels
>   on the white table and waited."

But the year I was five, my right foot
was almost out the screen door
for the green backyard

when I was swept up like a house in a tornado.
It will be over soon.
I lay on cold metal
with a washcloth over my face.
Breathe deep.

And ether kept me motionless on the table.

Orchids

My mother is watching them go past the car window.
They are small, a scrim of pinkish lavender
in the tall grass between the road and the papaya trees.
She is wondering what they are, growing from cinders
black as the coal her father used to mine.
The air is hot.
We are on the other side of the world from the kitchen
where the owner of the mine
gave her the large finicky purple kind.
He is dead now.
She never married him.
Or had another child.
She is wondering how orchids can grow wild like this,
open to the sun and the northeast trades,
their roots in a volcano,
their heads nodding and nodding on the asphalt shoulder.

The Horses at Hanagita

Down the sunlit shaft of the Cessna's wing,
I see their browns and blacks on a blaze of gold.
Abandoned when the hunting camp shut down
because this is Alaska Monument,
eight horses refuse to leave.

They want to be wild,
step past the gate of the open corral,
the single tent left shining like a patch of snow
on the shore of the lake.

Their necks curve under the coppers of poplar and birch.
They nuzzle in thickets of lowbush cranberry,
Labrador tea.
One bay is memorizing the names of the grasses.

They are so small in the blueberry fields.
Seven hundred feet above, I think of their hooves
in the pawprints of grizzlies,
how the dun's mane matches the tundra.

Soon they'll sleep in cradles carved
between mountains.
At the edge of the glacier they'll turn white,
begin the run downriver.

The steelhead I hook will be part rock,
part ice,
part leaping horse.

Northern Lights

Once more it's the rainbow leaps
and foldings of the old process,
a whole border of pink roses
growing wild on the horizon.

I remember those green and vermilion
hummingbirds never seen at this latitude
whose mating display took them higher
than tops of hundred-year trees.

Now these protons and neutrons
blowing down from the sun
to flow in the solar wind
like fish in a current.

When they enter the world's old breath,
oxygen, nitrogen,
instantly new shoots burst out
of the darkness.

Sometimes there's sighing
or a sound like rain on the roof.
Sometimes hooves of caribou herds
heading north in a single migration.

Charms against Bears

Walking through hardaxe red with the first cold slash
of the wind's claw,
Kip says carry a white stick. (His joke.)
If a snout pokes through,
carry the white stick faster.

Jina rings reindeer bells, steps
to the plane's pontoons shaking
the leather strand at paws of glaciers,
dens the shadows build in mountain rocks.

BEAR NAILS BEWARE
says the sign on the cabin door
in paint a lowbush cranberry red.
Across the entrance,
two-by-fours padlocked to steel.
And through them points of nails
shining like teeth or stars
in the night – Big Bear, Little Bear,
going away, coming back,
going away, going away.

No one carries a gun.

Wanting blueberries for breakfast pancakes,
I climb through silver and flame
to the shaggy patch where each is the eye
I'm not sure of under a lid.
I kneel to pick.
Indian women struck stones on cooking pots,

made noise run up the gullies
to frighten what frightened them.
I too have faith in the homely.

Bear, bear,
this is my thudding heart.

Ermine

All night the colors
come in the wind.
Each morning another birch wakes up
to its house on fire,
more willows run up the hill
with candles in their branches.

Joe's hands turn red dipping
the pail in cold lake water.
Another day and another,
blue will be ice.

He gathers breakfast scraps,
tail ends of bacon,
the last of the blueberry pancakes,
scrapes the heap near a stump
where the ermine hides
and waits.

Furtive is one word, sly
stepping of paws,
brown one and brown one
taking what's left.

Quick is another.
At six the sun goes down
like this,
doesn't hover,
grabs orange and purple,
drags all the light under.

Then the ermine gnaws
in the dark. One morning
we'll wake to a world
gone totally white.

for Joe Kelly

Tebay Lake

Water goes everywhere and is not afraid.
It falls from high rocks
making a rope for its descent.
Its heart breaks at the bottom
but there are three trumpeter swans
floating and mending.
Like an animal it sleeps in grass
under moon and wind
then leaves the shape of whatever it is.
It slides under birches like the sun
under a cloud and comes out again.
When a bear splashes in, water's own
white paw flies up in the air.

See it lean now to the pail, slip in.
From the dipper it looks back
with my own face.
Water, don't quiver when I swallow.
One day I'll be silt you run over,
the willow root you unwind.

Diggers at Langley

He's in black – pants, shirt, tight as a gunfighter's.
He carries a clam gun, the metal tube like a sawed-
off piece of drainpipe.
She follows in jeans, under her left arm
a square of raw plywood,
in her other hand a green pail the right size
for a quart of strawberries.
They're the only two people on the tideflat.

Seen from the top of the bluff, wet sand
curves in fjords and reaches to the minus one point
five line.
The rest is seaweed, heaps of it suddenly
stopped mid-sway when the water ran out
to lie like sculptured continents.
They are standing near the Strait of Magellan.

He seems to be trying to decide where to dig,
walks with his head bent down and turning
from side to side
as if reading a huge letter.
Already he's rounding the tip of Tierra del Fuego.
She stoops beside him to drop the plank.
Her gauze shirt slides up her back.
Even from the high window I can see
the longitudinal sweep of her spine
like the keel of a wooden boat, its ribs bare
on the beach after much sailing.

But she is young
and he wants to give her the world

although it is only a bucket of sand through which
she searches with her fingers.

And you and I will stay until the water deepens
and the stars come out on their black globe
or do not.

Poem

Someday we will take this chance again,
glide in some kind of warm water
past the edge of an overhang and look down.
The sun will be building pillars of light
in just this kind of space all the way to the bottom.
If there is motion, it will be silent as this
in the current of guessing and not knowing.
When fear swims in our hearts we will once more
breathe the strangeness of air in the brightness of fluid.
All our old hurts will be rose, turquoise, citron, violet —
we will flutter our fins tenderly over them
like the leaves of a tree over the tree's shadow.
We will float a long way. It will be a gamble,
keeping our masks tight, our lips closed, our eyes fixed
on what is beyond us and in us and all around us.

Kapoho, Hawaii

Silent

You, like most mothers who have it,
will never tell the secret —

your daughter's hair a wild light running down the stairway and *One*

Hundred Years of Solitude striking your head,
all the wineglasses broken so each shard

shines up and enters you from the kitchen floor.
Last night you had a nightmare.

You were calling a name over and over
but no sound went out into the black air

past the clench of your teeth,
your trapped tongue. With

her fingernails she makes the mark of a lioness
on your left cheek, but you do not choose the bitter cress

and arrange it with other hurts in a white bowl.
You comb your hair over the scab and then the weal.

She bites your wrist —
this part is hardest,

to see your blood run over its own blue veins
and their tributaries, knowing how it begins

with the heart,
and not cry out.

Ultraviolet

Pinewoods at noon, the sky walking
among them in a blue striped shirt.
Or a grass stem as scepter, insect
wings on the tip breaking light
into all its labors.
Once a redwood, a madrona, and a pine
stood on a steep hillside
roped together only by gossamer.
I saw them rise in their glittering bonds.
And so the invisible goes straight to the bone.
And so we get up day after day like the sun.

Spider

Beginning at my car's left headlight,
a spider, pure white, newborn, so minute
it could be a dry snowflake if this
weren't September, anchors a tiny thread
on chrome and sets out on the first run
of its life by climbing into space.

Meanwhile, above the garage another space
traveler is casting a heady light
on the door handle so that many dazzles run
together. And in just one minute
of shine, the spider aims its thread,
gossamer from the abdomen, at this

landfall. Its six or eight eyes do this.
And (wouldn't you know?) the little space
I occupy suddenly has a thread
confining it — I'm doing some light
reading in the front seat: a not-so-minute
mechanic is trying to make the car run.

Now the spider's paired feet turn and run
into air as if on all the earth this
compound were its to build other minute
compounds in. The spinnerets grasp space
like palpable meat. Another light
cable, silken, several-ply, now threads

its way upward. The spider is both thread
and needle — together they make a running stitch that shimmers in the moted light

all the way to the antenna, then claims this
height for a more intricate design. Space
fills. Sun fills the garage. In a minute

the complex orb will appear, the minute-
ly crafted center toward which every thread
bends. Will the mechanic rise from his space
under the hood, say that the car will run?
How can I open the door and not break this
order? And where will the spider light

when I drag its thread through a green light
going home this afternoon, the usual run
made in minutes? Where will it try new space?

Night Flying

All the time the moon goes down
through the last houses of the sky.
I count friends. It is night on both coasts.
Over the prairie the pilot says nothing
as if absence of lights is nowhere.

It is three years ago.
You sip bourbon and think the two of spades.
I whisper spades.
You think the nine of hearts.
I say nine.
It is not a dream, these wings
from mind to mind.

And the window is black with snow falling,
here and there lights like a small town
late at night.
You turn in your sleep.
Some faint thing half awakens you.

I think the queen of clubs, the five
of diamonds,
flints, little sparks in the darkness.

for Henry Carlile

Gourds

Elsie, my friend age eighty-two, is down in her garden
on the corner of Sunset and Bell.
Where I am above her in the small plane's cockpit
is not on her mind.
She does not guess I sit beside a daughter
whose feet move mysterious pedals, whose hands
tilt the wheel of our air-propped fortunes.
Elsie holds shears for the phlox — of this I am sure —
and a hoe for her pumpkin vines.

The heart of a Murani is like unto stone
and his limbs have the speed of an antelope.
Where do you find the strength and daring
to hunt with them, my sister?

A Nandi woman whispered once in the ear of Beryl Markham,
later first to fly the Atlantic from England west.
In nineteen-twelve the young girl's hunt was earthbound,
wildebeest, warthog, reedbuck.
Only flamingos carried fire to Africa's sky.

Near the end of the century, on the edge of another
continent, my daughter and I fly over Sunset and Bell.
Heaven is divided between two gourds a Nandi woman brings —
above us the one of cow's milk,
beyond the gourd with the blood of a bull.

Tomorrow Elsie will tell me she saw in the sky
a plane as yellow as her fence-hugging squash blossoms.

Voyage

It is true
the sun dips its oar
sooner and sooner
into the black waters
of winter.
The dipping is the making
of winter,
each pull across the sky
lifting the prow
of the horizon.
In the slave hold
the cargo shifts:
rocks, sticks, brown grass,
gray people in gray wool,
mud, a little snow.
But it is also true
one immigrant woodpecker,
pileated,
circles the mast
of the maple tree.
He makes a light
of white and red
and black.
He fills dead branches
with the wind
of wings.

When You Play in the Undertow

at Orr's Beach after the farthest rock
on the reef, black and red lava,
turns the blue and green sea spit-white
and the swell, calling its cavalry,
charges so you fall helpless
on the steep black slope where the tide changes,
foam all around you,
your bathing suit's cups and crannies
full of volcanic cinders,
your sinuses full of salt,

if you don't plant your feet like old pilings
in the sand when the waves turn,
submarine ropes pull you out like a sledge,
your whole cargo of self slides down
to the opaque blue where the ocean deepens,
and you go under as the next swell lifts you
for the race toward shore,
your body the center of its heavy birthwaters,
your flesh the imperfect balance
between earth and sea.

Kahuwai, Hawaii

Two

Testimony

for J.S., who died

Ravine

Because he thinks she moves like water,
because water moves down from the clouds,
slides along oak leaves, twines three-ply
strings in clay runnels, because rain
has been falling for days and a gale
has swept a tree onto the street,
because he thinks she moves like water
and water has always run away,
he wants to hold it in his fingers,
because the storm moves in his whole body
and nothing can stop it, his hands
are around her throat as he drags her
into acacias and ferns, feels himself
slip inside her mouth because
he wants to keep floating forever,
and because she moves like water
he sinks his knife into the flesh
of her neck to make a red pool
he wants to bathe in again and again.

Coroner

I had to follow her blood to its worst destination.
She knew the way. I kept to shadows and bruises,
staying close to her jawbone, her blue lips,
the scrape on the right side of her abdomen.
There was a kind of trail, neither north nor south,
along her arms and thighs. I saw sunset's purple
and the green of marshes. I was a hunter.
But there was nothing in her vagina, an empty cache,
and the eyes that saw everything were cold and shut.

I sat a long time near the lake inside her mouth.
Semen glistened in the fluorescent light over the table.
Nothing moved. I slid my knife into her throat
the depth of the other blade because some memory
might seep from the artery he cut, because
I wanted her fractured larynx to speak again.
Now I can tell you she died twice, early and late.
I had a tape recorder with me and a map
of the human body. I was not lost. She was.

Her Husband

Once I thought I knew all about live oaks,
dead butterweed, black roots.
The murderer was winter but eventually
everything was saved.
Summers we spent among the resurrected.
I focused the Pentax.
She shaded *Sitka columbine* and *yarrow* with her hand.
All evening we catalogued wildflowers
and in the morning climbed higher
to find *Flett violet*.

Now I know a second nature,
camouflage of trees after a storm,
streetlights out,
one night superimposed on another like two negatives.
He waited behind branches,
his breathing so light it could have been
their sway.
I looked for something white, her umbrella
at the side of the road,
the bread she'd gone for.
I never slept.
In the morning, how can I say it,
I found her, yes, face down,
throat cut, blood slipped into the veins
of all those fallen leaves.

Sometimes I dream she still waits
under a right pine.
I'm holding a stalk of crimson *paintbrush*.
Her body is taking the color.

Victim

Then the last being fell away from my face into the blindness
of shadow.
On my tongue words took the shapes of semen.
I was bruised all over, but I opened my eyes one final time.
There were the ferns.
There was the oak tree dripping rain.
I confused the shine near my throat, its sharp edge,
with a difficult ridge in the Sierra, some escarpment....

And where is the tangible part of me?
Torn blue jeans and tangled white nylon underpants
in a brown paper bag.
The district attorney asks my husband to identify my green
down jacket, blood crusted at the neck.
Poor man. He touches the label.
He brushes his cheek with the back of his hand.
He steps down.

And I am long since gone into the sad prison of emulsion
and paper.
I stare forever from police photographs,
the struggle, the long cut,
                    not knowing why I am here.

Beside Her Husband

We sit in the courtroom's semidark
as in a far northern dusk,
the sun poised endlessly on the rim
of the windowsill.
Over and over her body flashes to the screen.
She is lying face down under an oak,
one leg drawn slightly up
as if she might start to run again.
Or her left arm reaches out for leaves
or ferns or hands.
Someone has turned her over now
like a page in a book.
The knife cut is the color of plums,
blood darkening across her throat.
"How can you watch?" I whisper
when the camera shows the zipper torn
from her jeans,
her underwear twisted like a rope,
the thatch of pubic hair.

I remember once it was my body
the defendant fell on like a hawk,
and the brown mice of my fear.
I knelt. I wept.
I could not die bravely.

He answers, "I look at the floor."

Her Husband, to Himself

Cyanide and sulfuric acid: the smoke curls up
around his shackles, shrouds him for his grave.
His face vanishes in a green haze.

    During recess the bailiff chats with him.
    The beast smiles. Hands that let my wife's
    blood out of her throat are two dark rabbits
    in the hutch of his lap. He crosses one foot
    behind the other like a schoolboy.

In a room with several doors, the one in the floor
drops open. His neck snaps like a branch in a storm.
Four rifles aim at a white moon pinned to his chest
where his heart's last night is waiting. His flesh
singes with two thousand volts.

    His ears have another blackness. Into it,
    his attorneys whisper the pure light of the law.
    They have made him comb out his dreadlocks
    and shave his small goatee. He wears a maroon
    sweat shirt while my wife dresses in blue eternity.

Gary Gilmore, Jesse Bishop, Steven Judy,
John Spenkelink, Frank Coppola, Charlie Brooks...
The executioner always wears a hood. The ax gleams.
Blood spurts where his testicles slice off.
Behind the eyeslits it is always me.

His Mother

The night I wrapped the baby in a rag and ran away,
moonlight's blade slid right through the door.
The house was one long room like a shotgun
and the bullets were us, waiting for our deaths inside.
One last time, I turned to look at the boy
where he whimpered in his sleep,
the floor rubbing his welts.
And the girl behind the stove like a pile of sticks.
Later I heard their daddy took the wheels
off his new wife's wheelchair.
Two thousand miles away under the hot California sun,
I thought of him drunk on antiseptic,
cutting the willow twigs, braiding a whip.

Soot poured through the windows of the train.
Halfway to Mississippi, I got off somewhere,
cactus blooming and a moon in the daylight sky
like a vanilla cookie, to buy the girl a dress.
I wrapped it in brown paper. But over the sawmill's
whine in D'Lo I heard the boy teasing his goat.
Something else tied to a tree whose leaves keep coming back!
He watched her fingers slide under the string.
And the dress floated up all blue and white
like a cloud in the sky.
"Mama, you takin' her away from here!" he said.
The girl looked pretty, the two of us
skipping ties on the railroad track.

Yes, I went back for him too.
No, I don't remember the years.

They stack like wood behind the outhouse.
I brought his birth certificate. I said,
"This here you put in prison is only a child."
My firstborn, only boy, son of Charlie Red,

I took him last.

His Sister

At nineteen he was still signing his name
with an X.
The prison doors had already opened and shut
and opened again like eyes that don't forget.
I cupped his fingers under mine,
black skin to black skin.
Together we made the tall letters with shadows
and the round ones like tears.
On the dark path of his name there was no blood yet.

Then it was done. He looked down at the page
and saw his marks like bird tracks
in the mud beside the Okatoma.
"That's you," I said.
I wanted him to fly.
Again and again we traced his loops and hooks.

D'Lo, de l'Eau

He walked almost every day by water.
Below, the city on flatland lay stone on stone
to reach for heaven.
He was more near on the hill among dark pines,
the dog *Duchess* taking the little rain-created
torrent in great gulps.
That autumn,
prison was across the bay.
From across his lifetime came the slender song
of water
he took for solace between one unhappiness
and another.
He remembered his head on a woman's breast
in a town named for water.
He was born there.
He was borne away.

Another Witness

The prosecutor wants me to open
my memory like a trunk,
pull out the dress of India cotton,
green and yellow print
like a field of regimented flowers,
and slide its looseness over my head.
He wants the judge to see me wear
old bedroom slippers,
brush the color *mulberry*
on a windowsill,
the jury to hear a sewing machine begin
when the electricity comes on again.
A lineman touches wire to wire.
The doorbell rings.
The jury sees me running up the stairs —
I think the mailman has a gift.

                        But it's you,
thirteen years younger than you are now,
sitting between your two defense attorneys.
The floppy black felt hat you wore
that day when you asked to haul
the tree a storm blew down
is gone. Twice gone.
I almost say *hello*,
but you're too quick.
You grab my throat.
The lost crystal world of the chandelier
sways above my head.
No one hears the scream
I swallow when your hand

shuts over my mouth.
The other grips my hands behind me.

                    And I am so light
with fear you push me down the hall easily,
so light I float above the bed.
You pull me to my knees,
mutter an incantation behind my back.
Two gloves fly over my head.
You lift my dress.
Something feathered, a wren or winter thrush,
stirs between my breasts.

                    Now I must say it.
The word *sodomy* forms on my tongue,
dissolves like a wafer, forms again
to hang over the court reporter's desk.
A juror coughs.
I say *no*.
Oddly, you obey.
I think you have a knife.
When you enter the other place
I feel tears start.
The whole courtroom is silent.
Beyond the windows, Lake Merritt
shines in the sun
and joggers color its shore.
But I run back through time
until my thighs are sticky with you.
Don't tell, you say.
Thirteen years later

                    seventy-five people
turn toward the witness stand.
They see your limp hands on the bed,
a shred of noon light.
I kiss one knuckle. I don't know why.

The skin is sad and black.
A vein splits into two separate rivers.
I love you, I say into that air
                            and this.
Your palms stroke my face,
vanish like birds into a tree.
Don't move, you say.
Surely the blade poises
over my back now.
I wait to die.
Don't move, you say again.
The door shuts
                    and you are here
listening to how I wash my legs and face.
I change my dress, put on another,
rose and blue.
Outside, the street is a ribbon
tied to anywhere.
I drive an hour. Two.
I drive all the way to a telephone booth,
a police station, a lineup,
to another district attorney.
I drive to a different state
and back again
                    while you break rock in prison.
"Is the man you describe in the courtroom today?"
the prosecutor asks.
"Yes," I say.
"Will you point to him, please?"
When we face each other
                            she becomes visible,
the woman you murder twelve years
after me.

Her name is the same as mine.
Rain nets the hills.
Wind hurls a tree to ground
and lines sag without power.
She walks near that house
I left years ago, white shutters
and bricks unchanged.
One of us must lift her now
from the wet grass,
sponge clean her bloody throat,

                        I who spoke love,
                        you who killed for that lie.

Detective

I was in plainclothes, driving a car marked only
by late winter's mud. I thought clues would be hiding
inside the raped woman's house, bruises on her throat
in thumb circles or a spot like a crusted-over moon
shining from her dress. But a black man paused
near her hedge, his dark cords and navy watch cap
such as she described. He was wearing gloves.

The story is old now, obscured by murders,
but if I had accelerated up the hill
into Monterey pines, I think his steps might have
turned to her door. Of course, I picked him up.
He sat in the rear seat behind the police car's
steel mesh like a zoo animal. His face turned stone.

What lay in the palm of one glove was lipstick,
hers, as the laboratory proved later.
The print was of a slightly open mouth, caught
before the scream. It slept there in the empty
shape of his hand, the kiss he'd always wished
to awaken, although fatal.

Prisoner

The water speaks in all its slippery tongues —
Melanie, Margaret, Melinda, Wanda, Tish.
San Quentin above shows a single cell of sky
through the open manhole. He doesn't look up,

wants only the sewer's dark where his feet
swing down the limbs of iron footholds.
This is how he is free with orders from Maintenance
and a wrench for the penstock valve. This is how

he stands on a riverbank again, the arch of tile
his old bridge over flood. He doesn't mind the smell.
The water runs down to its purification.
He tries to remember the body it resembles most.

Notes

1. *Page 20.* Tebay and Hanagita lakes lie at the convergence of the Chugach and Wrangell mountains in Alaska, approximately one hundred air miles northeast of the Copper River delta. Accessible only by floatplane, they are now within the boundaries of the Wrangell-St. Elias National Park.

2. *Page 29.* "Gourds" was written after reading *West with the Night* (San Francisco: North Point Press, 1983), the autobiographical account of Beryl Markham's youth in Africa and her subsequent historic first flight from England to North America in 1936.

3. *Pages 35-50.* The poems in Section Two, entitled "Testimony," are based on the murder trial of Charles Jackson held in Oakland, California, in 1983. His conviction is under appeal at this time.

4. *Page 38.* The first lines of stanzas one and two of "Victim" were suggested by analogous lines in Robert Bly's "Poem on Sleep."